IN THE LATE,
DARK,
DEEP OF THE NIGHT

Miyerra Kindergarten

Christmas 1998

Published in Australia in 1994 by
Koala Book Company
Unit 1, 722 Bourke Street, Redfern,
New South Wales 2016, Australia.

Devised and produced by
Tucker Slingsby
27 Bockhampton Road, Kingston upon Thames,
Surrey KT2 5JU, England.

Text and illustrations copyright © Gwenda Harslett-Jeffrey and Julie Beech 1994
This edition copyright © Tucker Slingsby 1994

All rights reserved. No part of this publication may be reproduced or transmitted
in any form or by any means, electronic or mechanical, including
photocopying, recording, or any information storage and retrieval system,
without permission in writing from the copyright holders.

Designed by Mick Wells

Printed and bound in Singapore

ISBN 1-875354-85-9

IN THE LATE, DARK, DEEP OF THE NIGHT

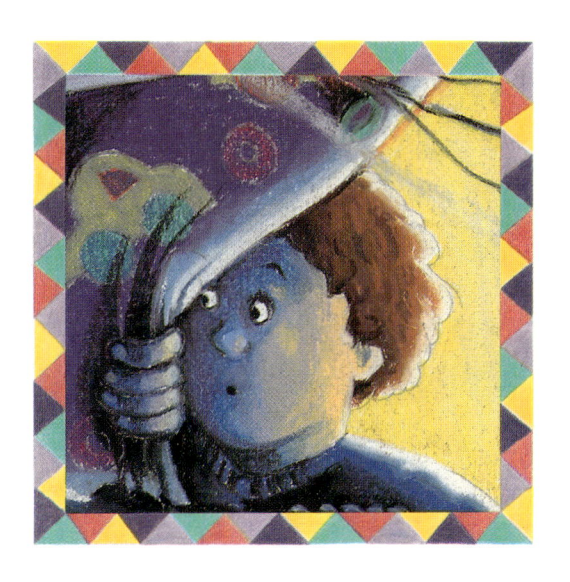

by
Gwenda Harslett-Jeffrey
Illustrations by
Julie Beech

KOALA BOOK COMPANY

In the late, dark,
deep of the night,
something woke me
with a fright.

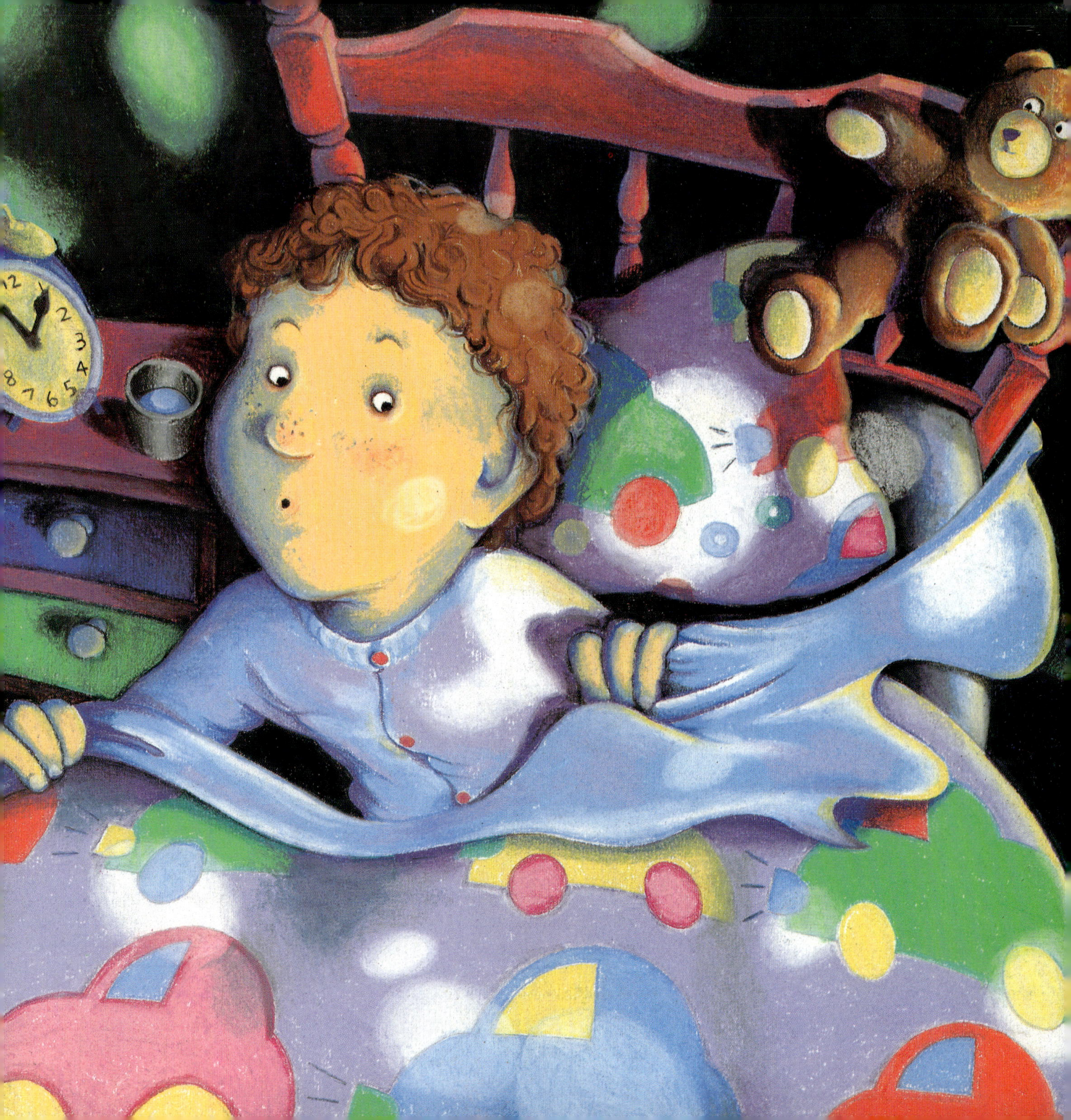

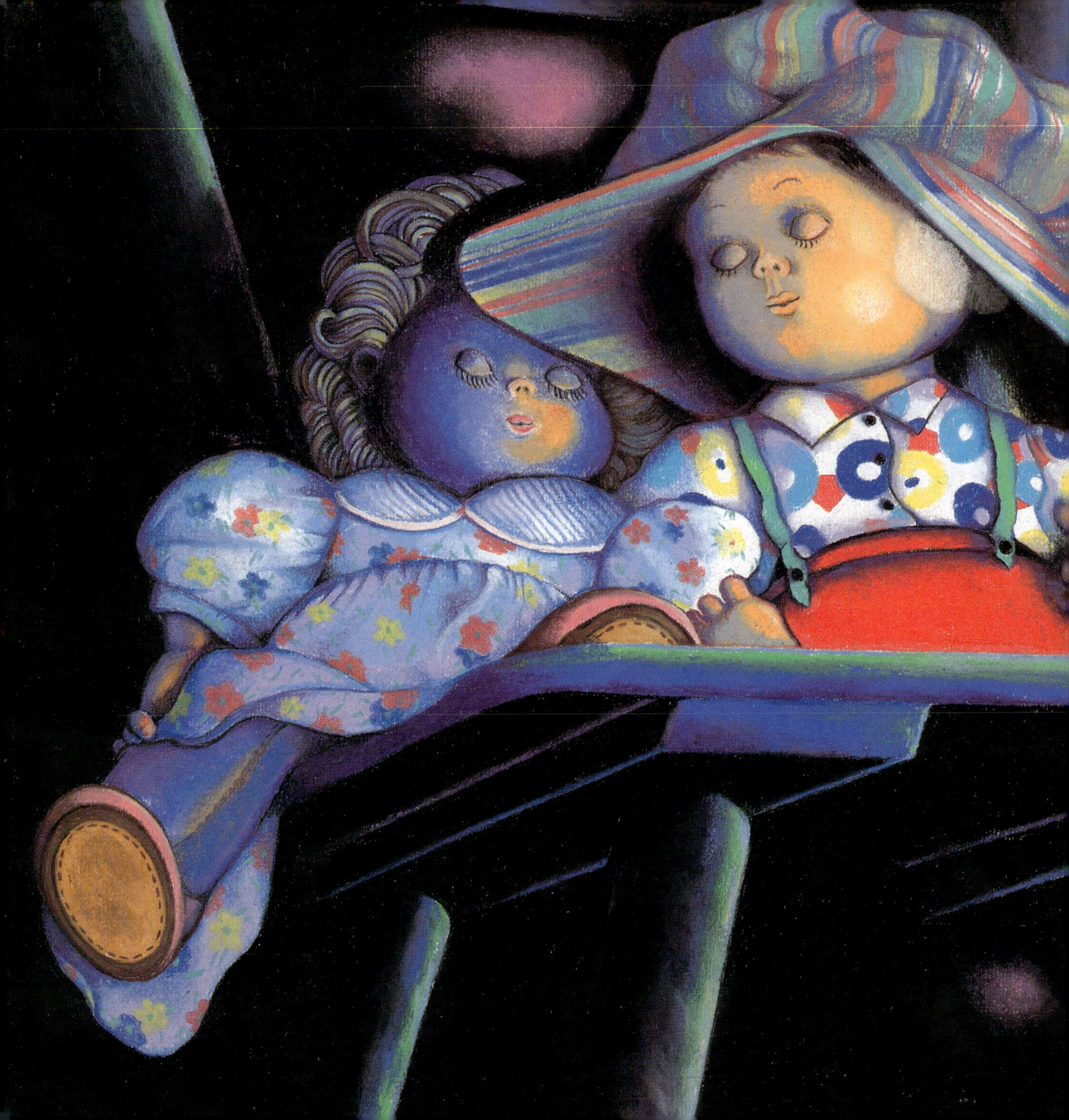

It isn't girls;
it isn't boys.
They don't make
that kind of noise.

It isn't the wind
in the trees out there,
it's not a wolf
or a big brown bear.

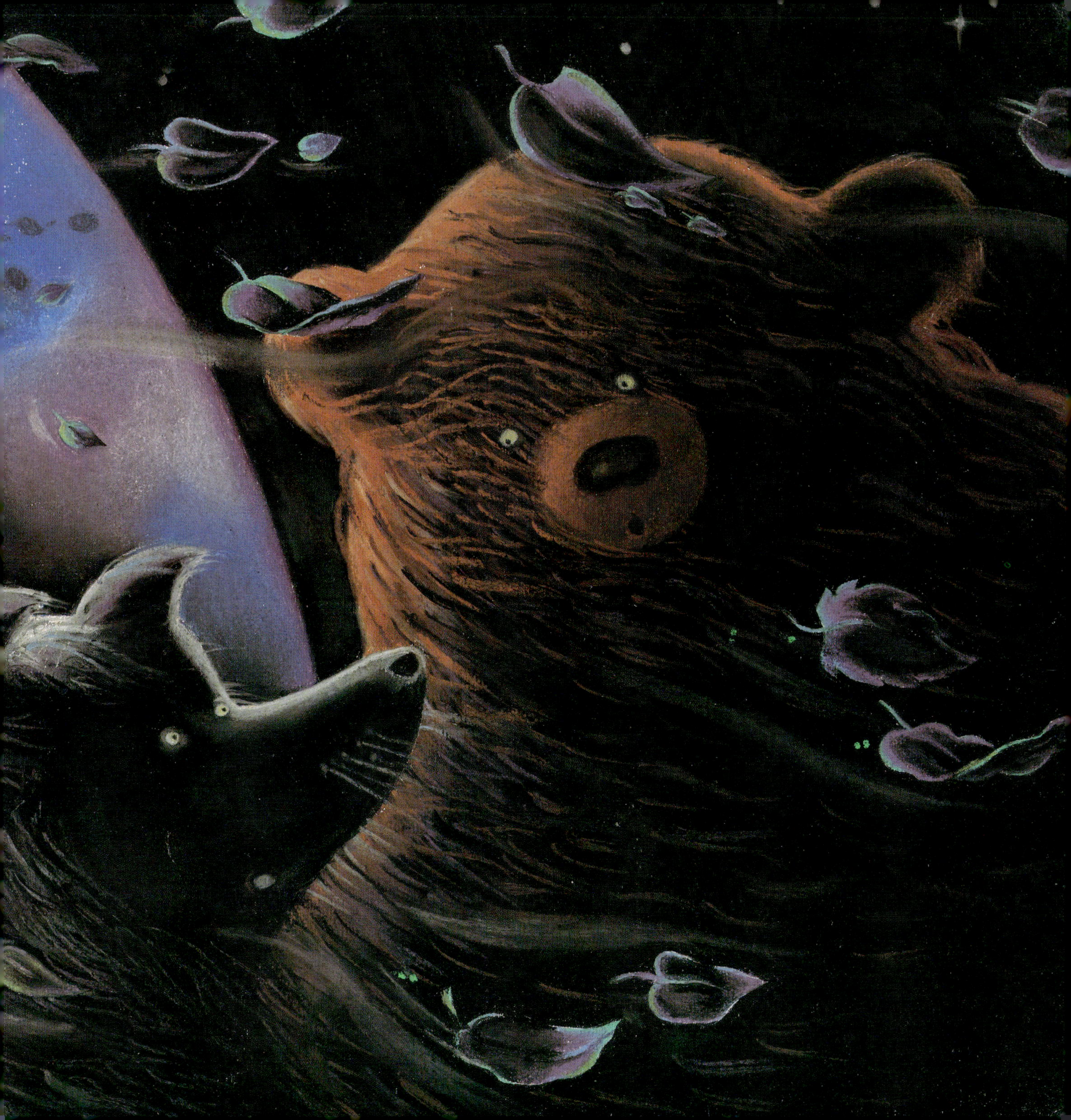

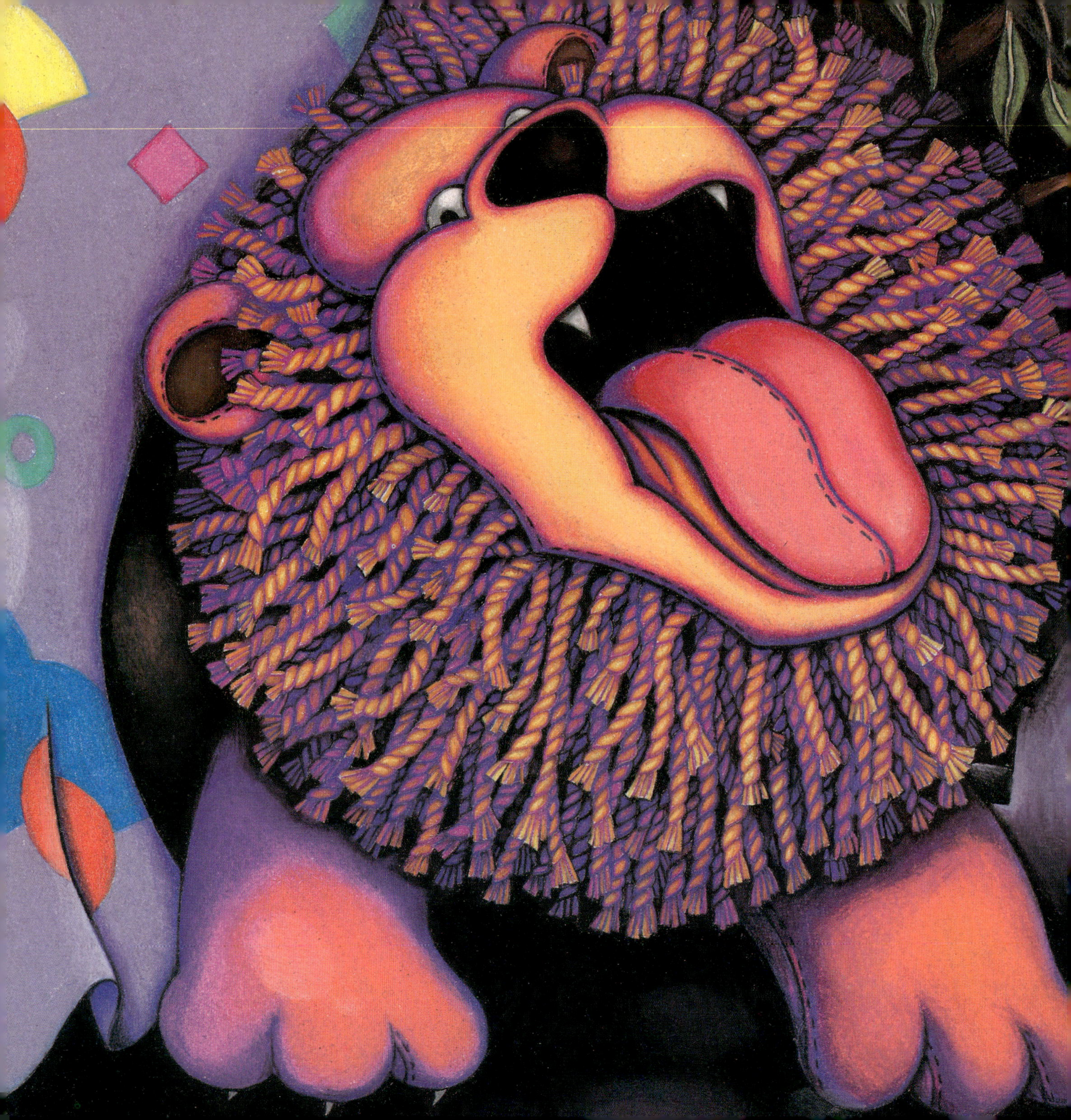

It doesn't sound
like a lion's roar
or Mr Maloney's
circular saw.
(Mr Maloney's the
man next door,
and he's asleep
in his bed I'm sure.)

It's a scary noise.
Could it be
a pesky possum in
the big gum tree?

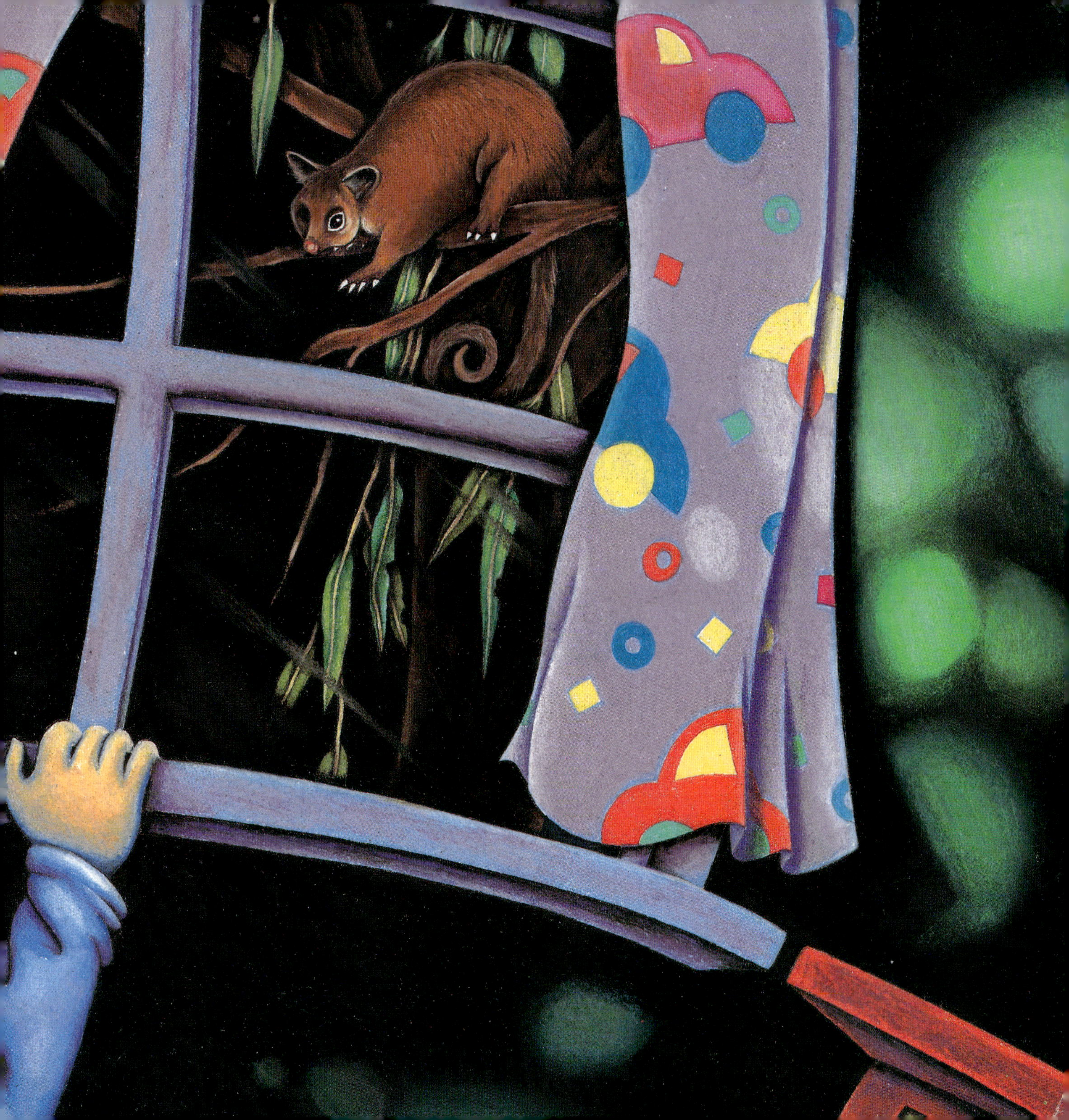

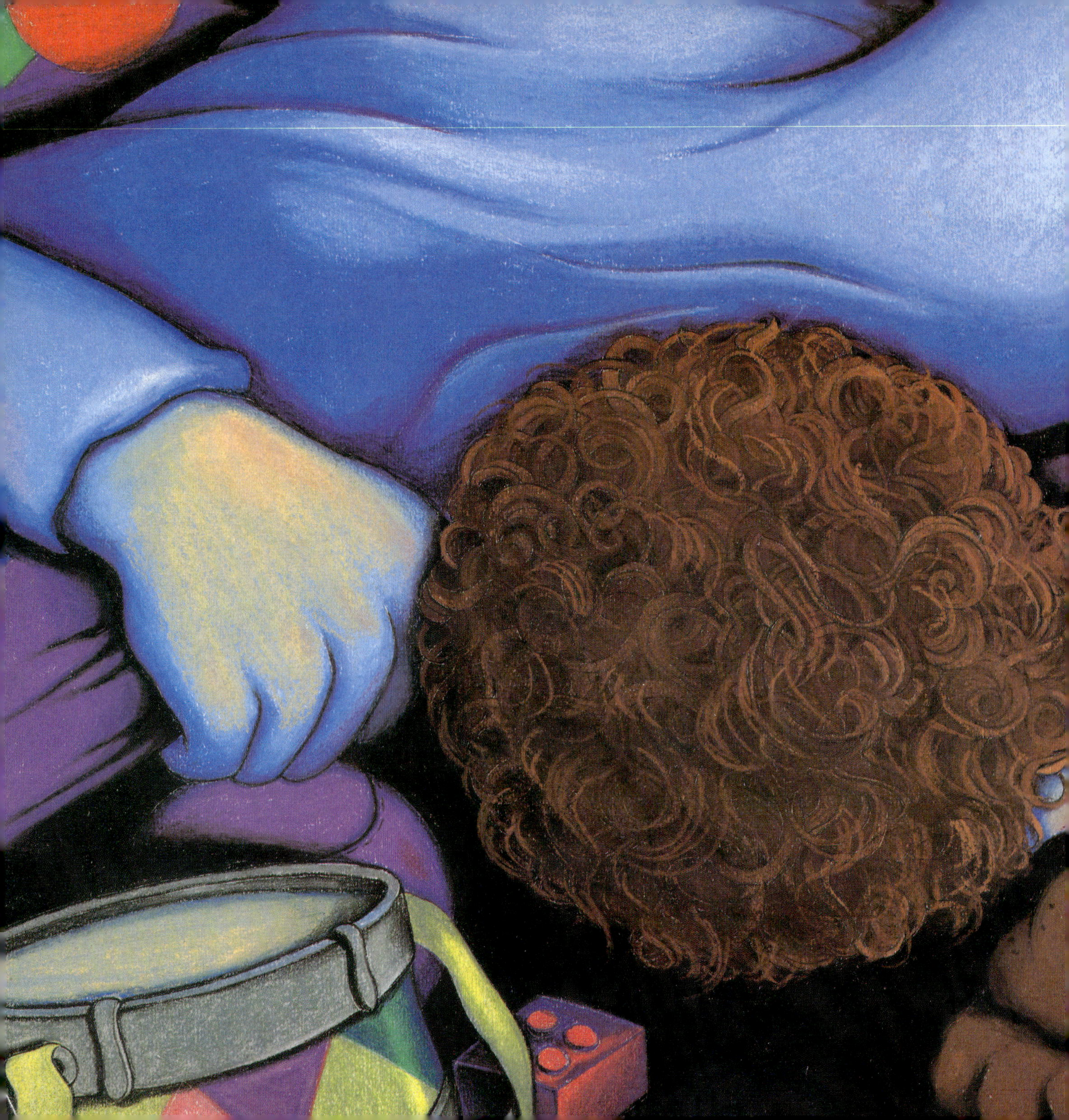

It's certainly not
a dog or cat;
the noises they make
are not like that.

It's not the sound that thunder makes, and the roof doesn't squeak and the ground doesn't quake.

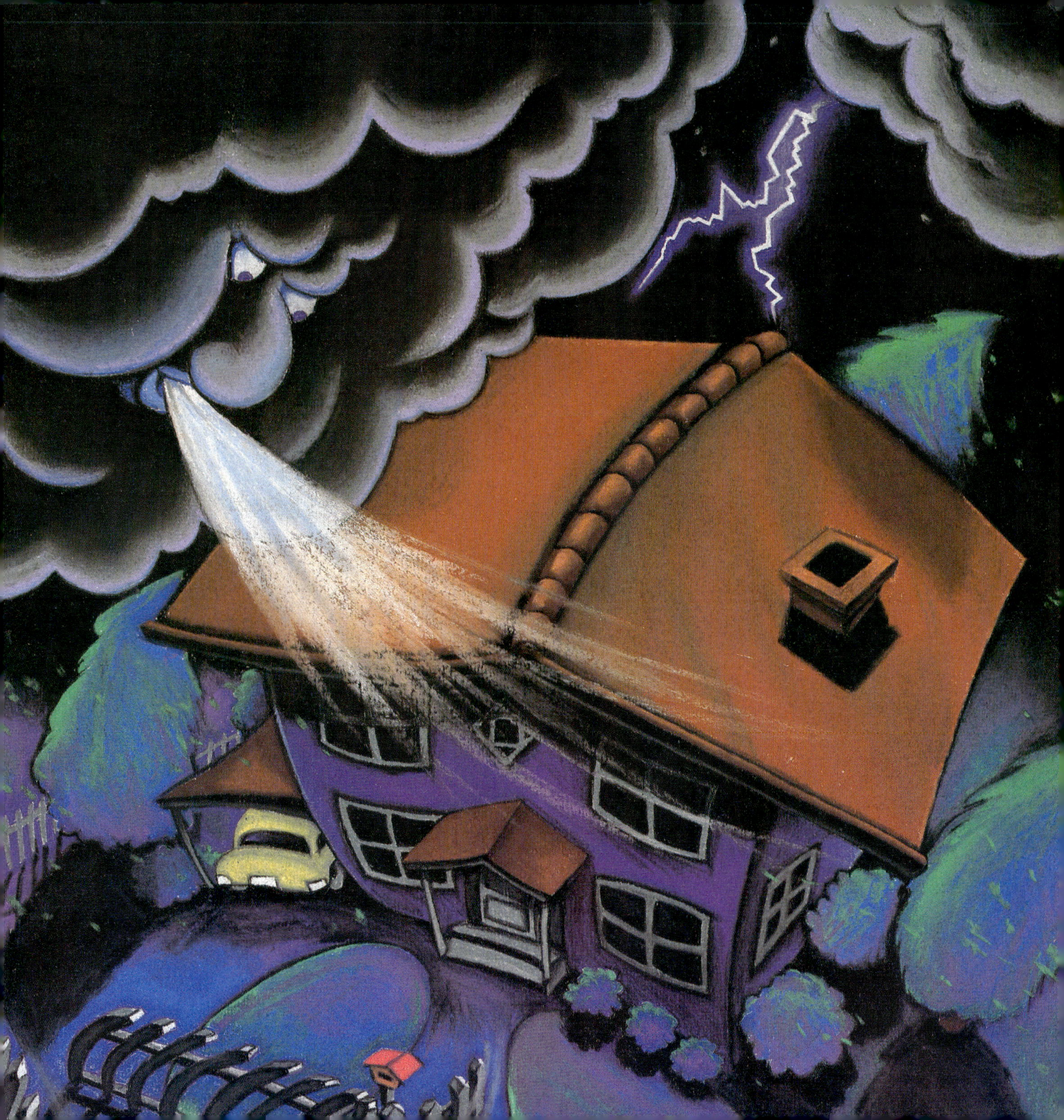

It isn't the sound
of waves of the sea;
I know it's not that,
so what can it be?

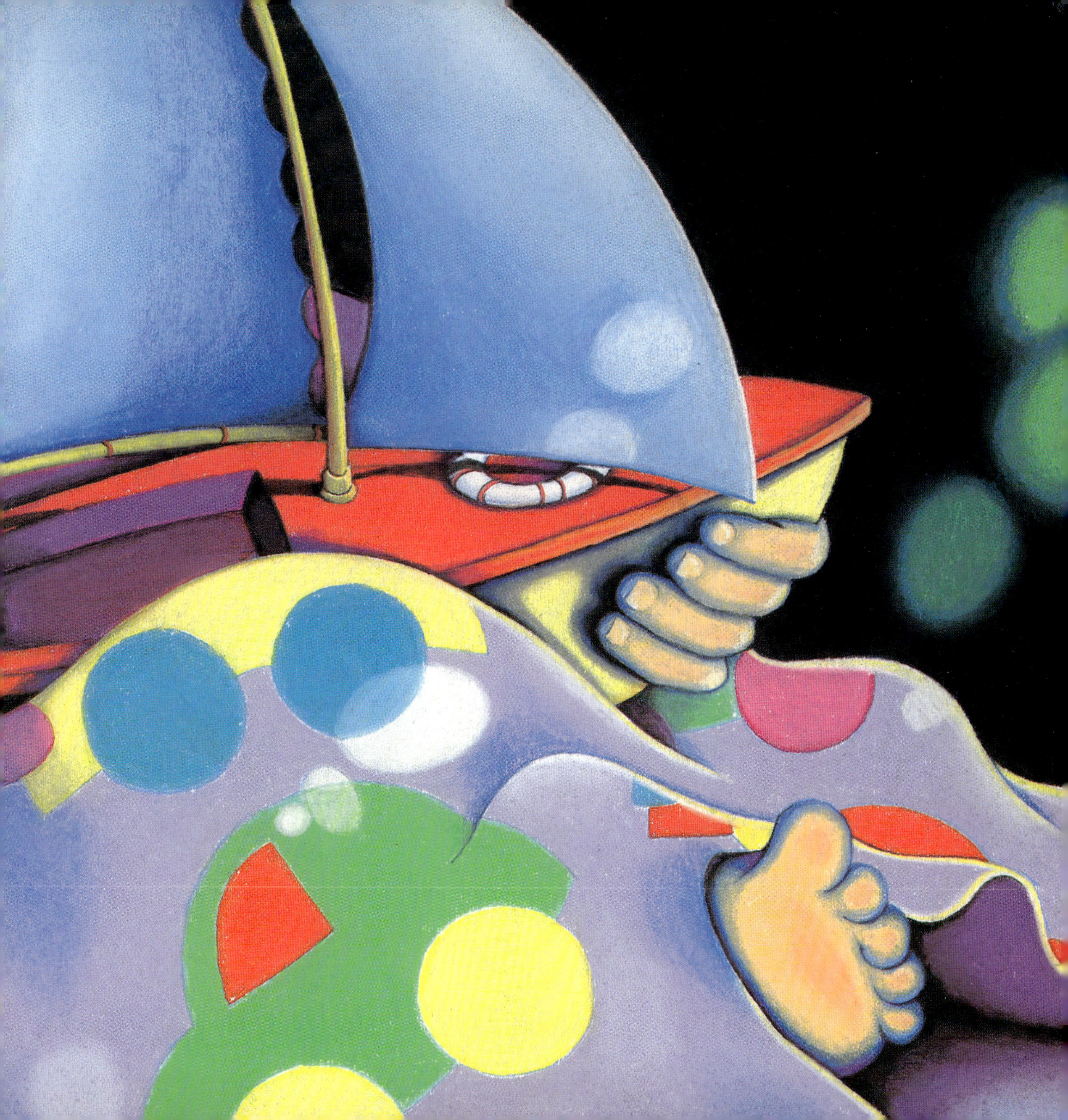

I'll tiptoe up
to my Mum's door;
she'll tell me
what it is I'm sure.

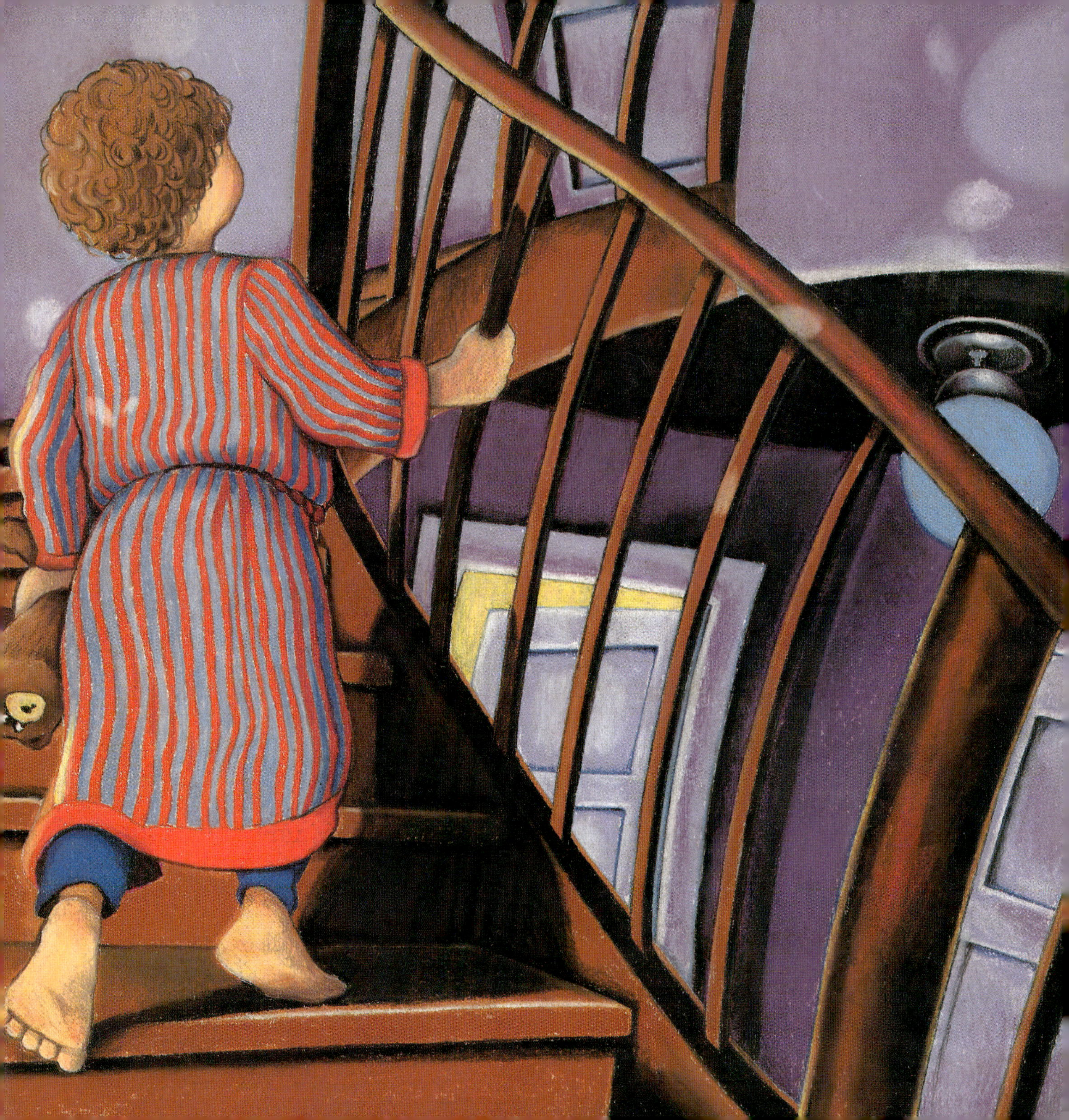

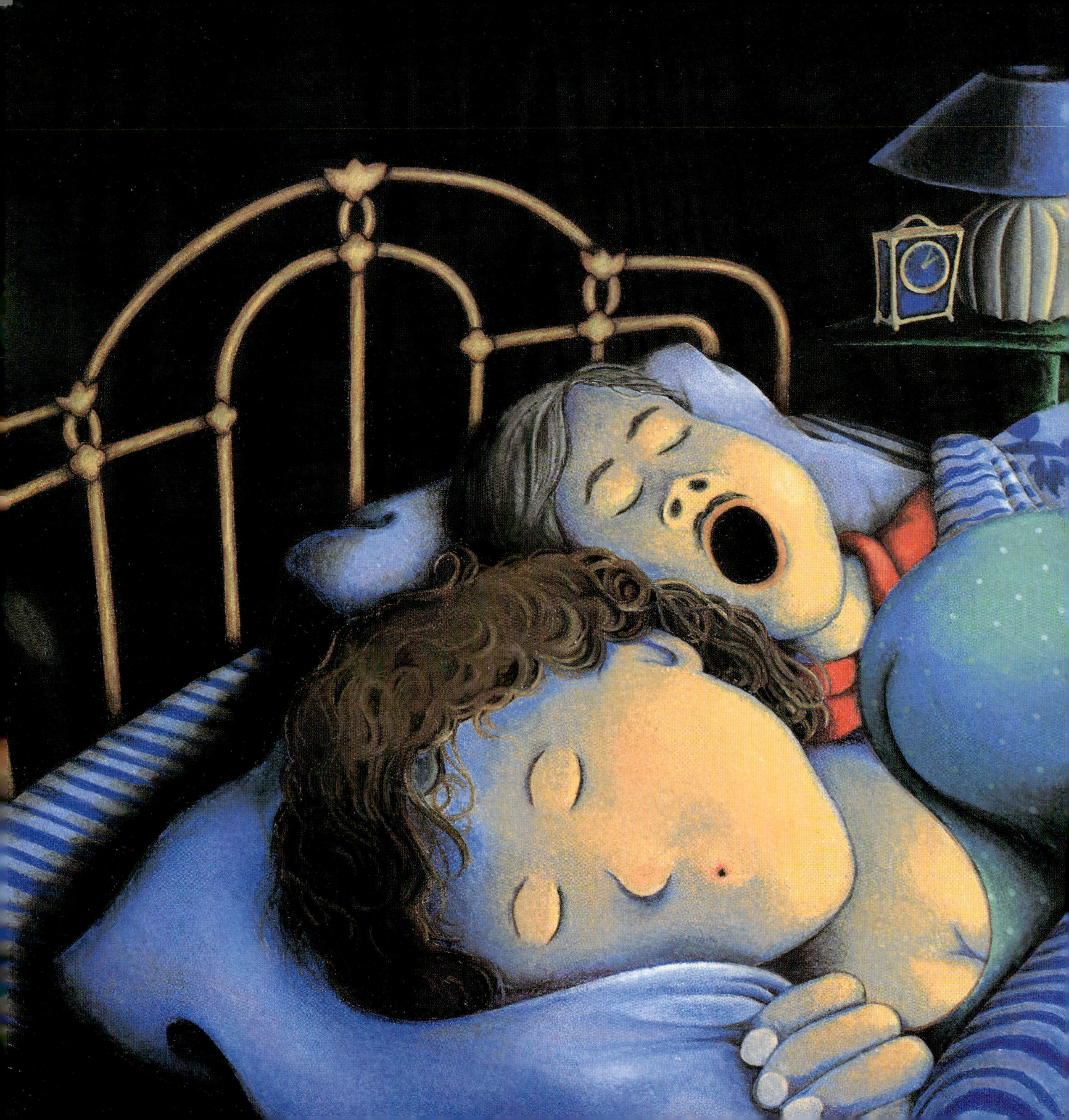

Well, there's my Mum
and at her side,
is Dad. His mouth
is open wide.

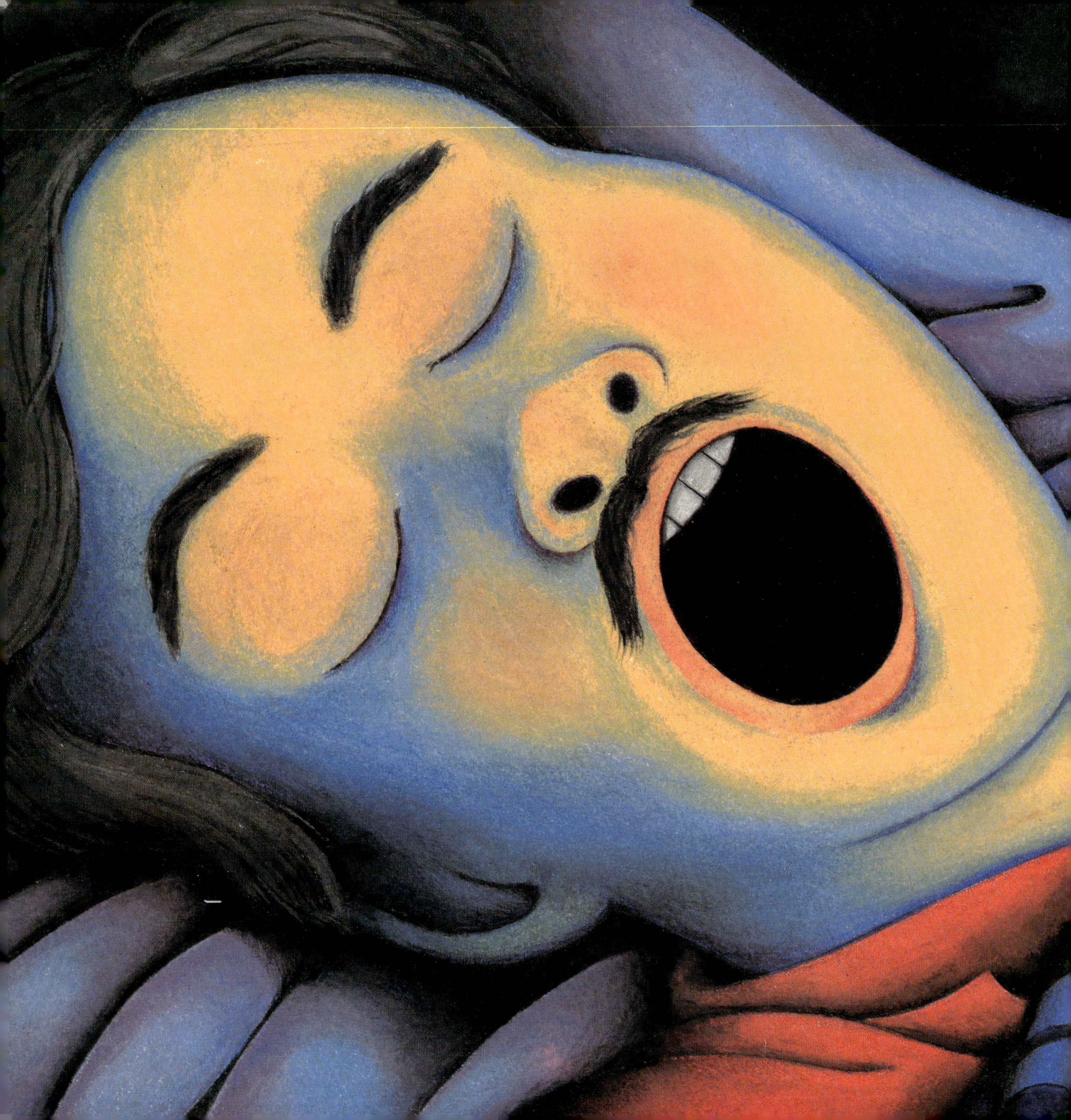

And from his mouth
a hideous roar
and a suck and a
whistle and then once
more...

I think I'm going
back to bed.
I'll pull the sheet
right over my head.

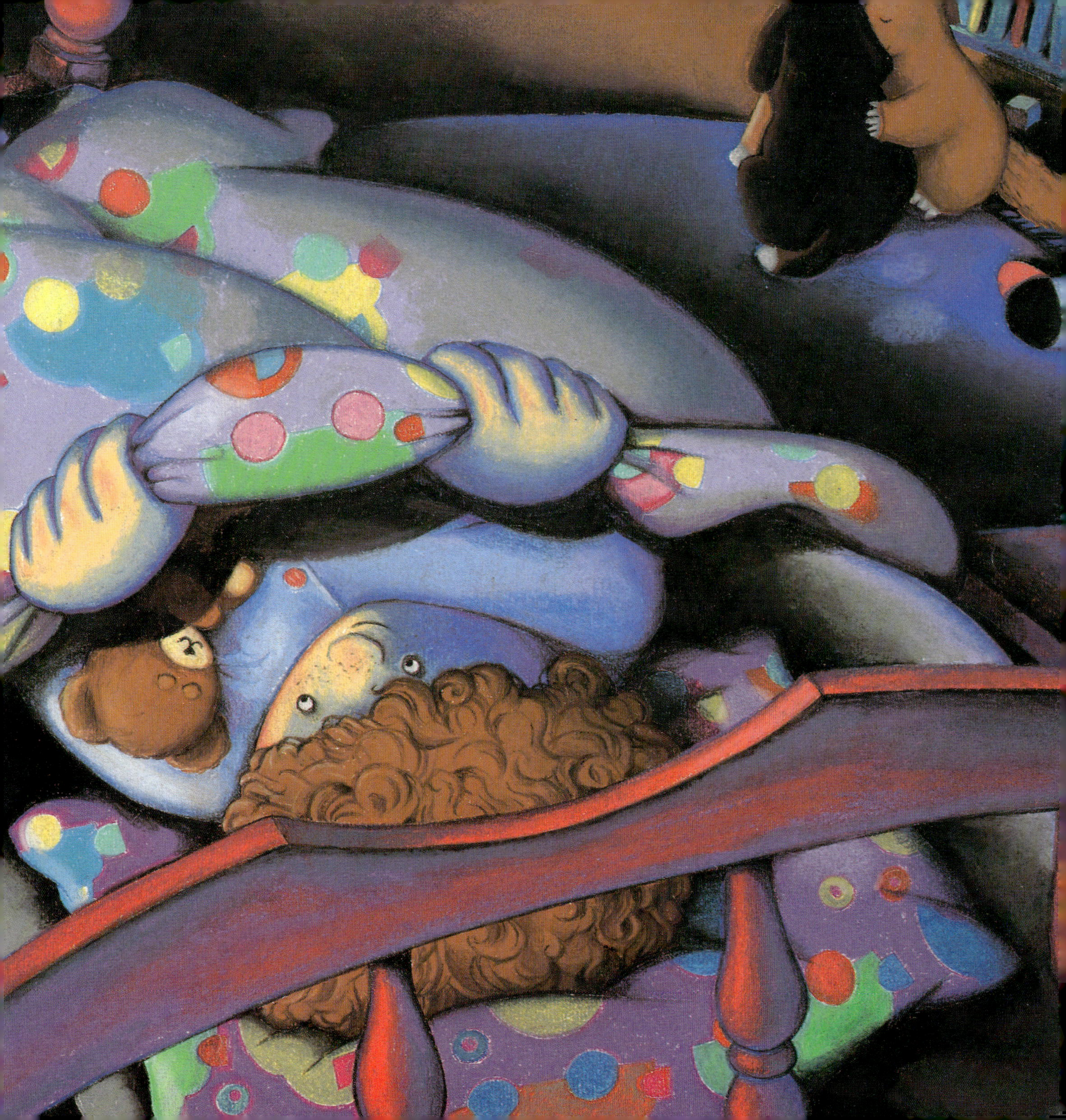

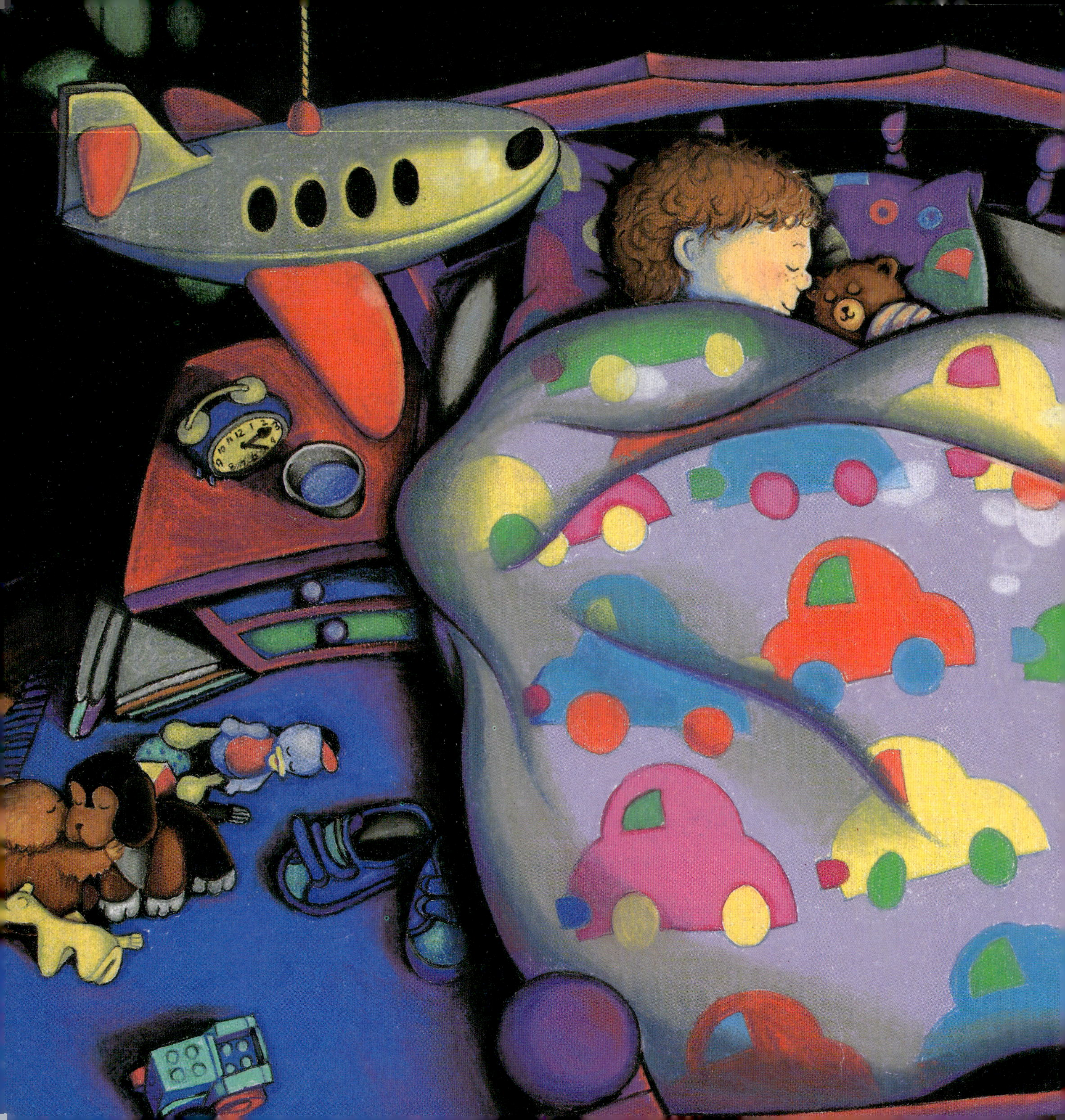

I don't fear
THAT noise I hear:

That's snoring.

How boring!

The end